To Rise Again

After wandering the desert, Roserin and her son thought they found refuge in Farona. But priests there kidnap Sethin in the middle of night and send Roserin on an impossible journey to save him.

Firestone

At the mercy of a tyrant and his sorcerers who covet the gemstone and its power, Jorane languishes in a dungeon cell, thousands of leagues separating her from the source of her own magic.

After more than three decades, storyteller and poet F.I. Goldhaber continues writing professionally. As a reporter, editor, business writer, and marketing communications consultant, she produced words for newspapers, corporations, governments, and non-profits in five states.

She wins awards for her fiction and poetry. Preditors & Editors readers poll ranked her second poetry collection, *Pairs of Poems,* third internationally. Various organizations honor her erotica works. Her short stories, novelettes, poems, news stories, feature articles, essays, editorial columns, and reviews appear in magazines, ezines, newspapers, calendars, and anthologies. She also published five erotica novels under another name.

In addition to paper, electronic, and audio publications, F.I. shares her words at events in Salem, Keizer, Portland, Seattle and on the radio. She appeared at venues such as Wordstock, Oregon Literary Review, bookstores, libraries, and Chemeketa Community College; gives presentations on subjects as diverse as marketing, writing erotica, and building volunteer organizations; and taught Introduction to Indie Publishing at Portland Community College and as a weekend intensive.

http://goldhaber.net/

Table of Contents

To Rise Again 1

Firestone 23

To Rise Again

Fantastic Worlds Publishing

ISBN: 978-1-937839-23-9

Copyright © 2014 by F.I. Goldhaber

Fantastic Worlds Publishing
http://fantasticworldspublishing.com
P.O. Box 80766
Portland OR 97280

Acknowledgements

Many thanks to all those I have learned from through the years, especially the Wordos professional writers workshop and Larry Brooks. Thanks also to those who have freely shared their knowledge online notably Dean Wesley Smith and Kristine Kathryn Rusch. Those who inspired me to pursue writing from an early age include Ruth Wright my fifth and sixth grade teacher at Randolph Elementary School in Huntsville, Alabama, Nancy Travis my freshman English teacher at Clear Creek High School in Texas, and most prominently my parents, Jerry and Bev Goldhaber. Very special thanks to my editor, Laurie Lawhon of Fine Tune Your Words and my beloved husband Joel Goldhaber.

To Rise Again

Sometimes legends take flight, but at what cost?

F.I. Goldhaber

To Rise Again

By F.I. Goldhaber

Metal pounding on wood woke Roserin and she bolted upright. Sethin fully opened the damaged door and she saw half a dozen black-robed priests, their faces covered by their cowls, standing in the dark lane outside the adobe hut. Two of them grabbed her son by the arms and dragged the young man away before Roserin could get off the floor to stop them.

She pushed herself to her feet, grabbing a blanket to wrap over the thin fabric of her night-shirt, and ran after them through the streets. When she finally caught up with them — gasping for air, her heart pounding in her chest — one of the priests turned and held his bronze staff across his chest to block her passage.

"You cannot help him now. Come to the temple in the morning. Ask for Lukich. He will explain what you must do if you wish to save your son."

Roserin dropped to her knees in the dirt of the lane, sobbing. She had thought the village of Farona offered them refuge. After nine years of wandering from desert village to desert village, they had found people who allowed them to earn a meager living. Roserin leaned over and heaved, her stomach churning up bile. When the spasms stopped, she muttered, "I hope every one of Tsorak's priests burn in the lava pits of Nodegam for all eternity."

She fought the urge to go after Sethin. But no one in Farona disobeyed a priest's instructions. Not knowing what else to do, she returned to the one-room hut that huddled against the wall surrounding the village midden. In exchange for hauling waste out to bury in the fields, she and Sethin earned a place to sleep and enough food and water to survive.

After the priests' pounding, the door to their hut hung askew and Roserin did not try to close it, for the latch was broken. She pulled on her cotton breeches and replaced the nightshirt with a bodice. Her fingers trembled, making tightening and tying the laces difficult. With the blanket wrapped around her shoulders, she set off in the dark for the center of the village. She saw no one in the streets or in the huge square in front of the massive stone temple. Climbing the steps, she perched on the edge of the top one and waited for dawn, clinging to the hope that Lukich would offer her a way to save her son.

A sandal-clad foot touched Roserin's shoulder and shook her awake. She stood and faced a young man, his skin the color of the dirt, wearing the dark brown, hoodless robe of an acolyte. Without speaking, he turned and she followed him around the temple to one of several adobe huts behind it. Inside, a reed mat covered the floor and the acolyte sat down on it, crossing his legs. He nodded and Roserin joined him.

"You are Lukich?"

"Yes."

"Why did the priests drag my Sethin away in the middle of the night?" Roserin gripped the laces of her bodice, fighting to keep the anger and fear out of her voice. "He has done nothing to offend them or your god. We have asked only for a place to sleep and food to eat."

"Your son bears the mark of Tsorak under his eye."

Roserin hand flew to cover her mouth, hoping to prevent the priest from hearing her gasp. The small triangular mark had marred Sethin's pale face from birth, getting darker as he grew taller. When he reached puberty eleven years ago, the priests of Svinal, the god she had wor-

3

shiped all of her life, chased her son from the temple. The elders exiled them both from their village near the ocean, never giving them reason for their banishment.

Thereafter, wherever they stopped to seek shelter, priests ostracized them as soon as they saw the mark under Sethin's eye. But, until today, even in Farona, none had ever named it.

Lukich ran a hand over coarse black hair cropped close to his head. "On the equinox, the priests will sacrifice Sethin to Tsorak and beg the god to remove the poison from the lake."

Roserin heard wailing and realized it came from her own throat. She could think of no way to extricate Sethin in two days. She wanted to spit in Lukich's face. Apparently, the priests had only pretended to allow them refuge in their village.

"You can save him only if you offer your life to the god in exchange for his." Lukich stared at her out of eyes so dark they appeared black in the dim light of the hut.

"How?" Roserin's breath came in gasps. The priests had to know she would do anything to save her son, even die in his place.

The acolyte pulled a gilded box from the sleeve of his robe. "First, you must shave off your hair."

Roserin ran her fingers through long blonde locks. A tear crept down her cheek, but the hair her people treasured had no value here in the desert. And, she suspected the god wanted more.

4

Lukich placed the box in front of Roserin's knees. "Put your braided hair in this box and carry it up the mountain to Tsorak. There you must recite the prayers I will teach you and place this box with your offering at the god's feet."

"Why?" Roserin picked up the box and turned it over in her hands. Ivory inlay on the lid, yellow with age and polished so smooth she could not feel where the wood ended, depicted the phoenix god.

"Only a priest may approach the god with covered skull."

Roserin shook her head, looked up at him, and scowled. "Why did you capture my son? So you could coerce me into supplicating your god? What does it want from one who grew up in Svinal's service?"

The acolyte shrugged. "My grandfather told me tales of when he was a boy. Tsorak came to life and saved the village from drought. Then, too, a stranger had wandered into the village bringing with him a son who bore Tsorak's mark. That stranger summoned the god on his son's behalf. We need such a miracle again."

Tears streamed from Roserin's eyes. "What will you do to him if I do not carry this to your god?" She held up the box.

Lukich bowed his head. "At noon on the equinox, unless Tsorak rescues him, your son will burn to death in the temple square."

"No!" Roserin wailed again.

Lukich slipped his hands into the opposite sleeves of his robe. His expression remained impassive.

She sobbed. "What exactly must I do?"

After he explained the rituals and Roserin recited the unfamiliar prayers dozens of time, Lukich led her through a small entrance near the rear of the temple. They descended stone stairs into a narrow passage with doors on either side. A priest guarded one near the end. He stepped aside when Lukich approached with Roserin.

Lukich lifted the bar from the door and pulled it open. Roserin took a deep breath and stepped inside.

"Mother." Sethin's voice trembled in fear. He lay on the dirt floor on his side, his arms bound behind him.

Roserin sat on the floor, lifted Sethin's head into her lap, and stroked the silky blond locks that grazed his shoulders. "Lukich has explained what I must do to gain your release, my sweet. I leave at midnight to fetch Tsorak from the mountaintop to rescue you." She tried to keep her voice calm, but the terror in Sethin's eyes made her tremble. For the first time in two years, she spoke to him in the language she had taught him as a child. "Curse Tsorak and all Faronans for abusing you so. They should choose one of their own kind to sacrifice, someone who worships that stupid bird." She wrapped her arms around his shoulders and pressed her cheek to his. "I promise, my love, I won't let them harm you."

Roserin reached the lake at the base of the mountain by midday. She trudged along the shore, wincing as sand granules found their way over the tops of her worn boots to chafe at her heels. With her parched lips, the lake's waters looked tempting, despite the death that lurked there. Loosening her bodice laces, she let the dry air wick sweat from her skin. She brought the opening of her almost-empty water skin to her lips, taking just enough moisture into her mouth to ease the dryness. When she reached the top, she would reward herself with enough water to wet her throat.

Clutching the golden offering box, Roserin pushed at her knees, struggling as the grade steepened. She gasped for air and her sweat-dampened breeches clung to her legs. Young people found this journey arduous; rarely did someone who had lived nearly forty years attempt it.

Roserin hugged the mountain side of the narrow trail to avoid the crumbling edge and the sight of the steep, barren slope that fell to the lake shore. The sun beat down on her pale skin, blistering her bald scalp. The summer air did not move and Roserin yearned for a breeze, however slight, to cool her skin.

A snake slithered across Roserin's path and she jumped. The serpent, as thick as her arm and long enough to wrap itself around her several times, hissed and its tongue flickered in warning. Roserin backed away, but her feet slipped out from under her at the trail's edge and she found herself sliding down the slope. She grabbed at a rock with her empty hand and one foot caught on another, stopping her descent. Above her head, the snake coiled itself into a pile in the middle of the path. Her heart thumping in her ears, her fingers trembling, Roserin pulled herself to her knees. She tucked the offering box into her bodice and inched her way up the slope, scrabbling for handholds among the protruding rocks. By climbing at an angle, she reached the path several yards beyond the thick loops of the snake. It hissed at her again when she rose to her feet, but did not move toward her. She brushed off some of the dust and looked in dismay at the stinging scrapes on her hands and arms.

Roserin stayed alert for the rest of the journey up the mountain, watching for snakes and listening for the scritching of marmots. When she finally saw the stone phoenix towering over the bleak summit, Roserin wailed. The statue, more than twice her height, stood on a huge pedestal. Winter winds had whipped across the peak to wear away the carving's details. "How will a rock help my Sethin?" she asked aloud. "Where is the phoenix god?"

Roserin wanted to fling the offering box at the statue and scream her frustration, but she had not yet caught her breath from the long climb. After spending half the night and a good part of the day walking the long road from Farona to the mountain and then climbing the steep path, all she could do was collapse in the shade of the pedestal. She sucked a mouthful of water from her skin. She shook the bag. A drink or two more would empty it.

In her thoughts, she repeated every curse she had ever heard in her native language and in the Faronan's. For the two years she and Sethin lived in Farona, the priests had never asked them to pay homage to their god. Now, they apparently expected her to give obeisance to a stone statue. She could have spent these last hours comforting Sethin or looking for a way to rescue him from the guarded temple. Instead, she sat alone on the mountaintop seeking a miracle from a god made of stone.

Roserin stood and looked up at the phoenix. How would performing rituals for a piece of rock aid her son? No god would witness her deeds and the priests would not know what she did on top of the mountain. Roserin turned to head back, but hesitated. Although he had not told her what to expect, Lukich clearly anticipated something would happen if she followed his instructions. She had traveled this far in service to his false god. Saying the prayers might be Sethin's only hope.

Roserin knelt on the flat, dusty stone in front of the statue and recited the words Lukich had taught her. "Tsorak, I beg you to spare my son's life. I have brought you this gift." She set the golden box in front of the pedestal under the mammoth figure. "Your worshipers in Farona will sacrifice Sethin to you on the morrow in hopes you will then remove the curse that fouls the lake waters. Please, oh sage and sacred Tsorak, I appeal to your mercy." Her agony for Sethin resonated in her words. "Accept my gift. Take my life instead of his. I will do anything you require if you will show your priests in Farona that you do not approve of their choice and spare my son. Let Sethin live so that he can serve you."

Roserin stood and reached above her head to place the box where the great bird's statue met the pedestal. She opened it to reveal to the statue the thick, blonde braid that had hung down her back until last night. Then, she sat down again in the statue's shade. With her face in her hands, she sobbed, but her eyes did not have enough moisture to produce tears.

She had observed the rituals, but no god had appeared to rescue her son. She baked in the heat of the mountain unable to save him, unable even to comfort him in the last hours of his life.

Roserin looked to the edge and thought how easily she could jump from the precipice and end her own misery. *If I can't save my son, do I deserve to live?* Lukich had told her to offer her life to the god in exchange for Sethin's. But, he said nothing about her dying, nor did he suggest she needed to kill herself to save her son. If the god spared her son, she would serve it. If it removed the poison that had tainted the water for almost a year, she would join the Faronans in worshiping it.

Lukich said to wait until dark. Would the god appear at sunset?

When the shadow of the statue faded into the dusk and hot air no longer stifled her breath, Roserin heard stone grate against stone. Her eyes widened, her pulse quickened, and she struggled to her feet. She did not know which frightened her more, the possibility that Tsorak would venture down from its pedestal or that she stood in front of a lifeless statue offering no hope for her son.

A musty odor emerged from a dark space now open in the pedestal, and Roserin heard scuffling. But the last bit of sunlight had disappeared and she could not see inside. A cold mass weighted down one hand, and she closed her fingers around something with sharp edges that pressed into her palm. She heard the scuffling again, stone scraping stone, then silence. Another sob escaped her lips. Instead of a god who could fly to Farona and save her son, she only had a worthless bit of carved stone to show for her exertions despite Lukich's promise that the phoenix could rescue her son from a fiery death. She wanted to hurl what was in her hand from the mountain, but decided to wait until she could see what she held.

She must get back to Farona and her son. Nothing on the mountain would help him. She had to find a way to stop the priests from killing Sethin. Sliding one foot in front of the other, Roserin felt her way along the path. At last, the moon rose and she could see well enough to walk briskly. She opened her hand to find a small, onyx image of the phoenix god. *Who gave me this and why*? The statue had no value to her and Lukich had not mentioned such a thing in his tale. Still, if she gave the figurine to the priests, perhaps she could convince them they should accept it as a gift from their god and release Sethin. Roserin quickened her pace.

A snake slithered over her boot and she stumbled. She tried to regain her footing, but in the dim light she had strayed too close to the edge of the path. With a cry, Roserin tumbled over and over, rolling down the rough slope, slamming her knees, elbows, and head against the rocks. Bones snapped and Roserin tasted blood in her mouth. When her plunge down the mountainside stopped, the pain swirled over and around her.

Roserin could no longer feel her hands, legs, or back. A terrible ache swelled her head, cuts on her face stung, and blood poured from one ear into her mouth. She opened her eyes to see the onyx replica of the phoenix statue propped up against a rock near her nose, a crack extending from its beak to its talons. "If you take my life, Tsorak, you have accepted my gift. I expect you to climb off that pedestal and save my son." The stench of her loosened bowels overwhelmed the taste of blood in her mouth, and everything went black.

Roserin opened her eyes, but a thin, translucent membrane covered them and distorted her vision. She concentrated and the membrane slid to either side. The rocks, dirt, and scraggly shrubs near her still appeared a bit blurry, but in the distance she could clearly see the tower of Tsorak's temple at the center of Farona. She no longer lay on the ground, nor could she feel any pain. The sun climbed toward its zenith and Roserin's heart beat faster. Sethin had only until noon to live. Even if she ran the entire way, an impossible undertaking, she could not return to Farona in time. With the statue broken, she did not even have anything to offer the priests.

Roserin tried to move her arms and, with a shudder, unfolded the six wings now attached to her back and shoulders. Her breath caught in her throat. She blinked and shook her head, trying to clear her vision and her memory. Turning to look around from back to front, she rotated her neck nearly three quarters of a circle. Her mouth would only open and close, she could not form words. Talons had replaced her feet. Panic gripped her. She tried to remember what had happened the night before and wondered if she slept and this was but a dream.

Sethin. For his sake she must gain control of her fear and her body. If she had transformed into the phoenix, perhaps that gave her Tsorak's powers. Unfortunately, since she had paid only minimal attention to the religion of those she served, Roserin did not even know what those powers were. She thought about the poison in the lake, but she had no idea how a phoenix god would remove it. Lukich had said the god would rescue Sethin. First, she must save her son. Then, she could try to figure out what to do about the lake.

Roserin struggled until her wings beat against the air and lifted her above the ground. She dropped back down and almost tumbled over, unable to gain enough height. Repeating her son's name to strengthen her resolve, she finally coordinated her wing strokes enough to stay aloft. She could see the empty pedestal on top of the mountain. Shuddering, she wondered if she had assumed the bird's height as well as its form. The dreary landscape offered nothing against which she could measure her size. Somehow, large or small, she would find the strength to keep the flames from harming Sethin.

When he taught her the prayers, Lukich had

spoken of the god incarnate flying into Farona and snatching away the sacrificial offering. Roserin had given his story no credence, especially after she found only a stone statue at the summit. Now, she wondered about the purpose of her journey and the onyx figure given to her on the mountain. As long as she reached Sethin before noon nothing else mattered, she hoped.

Soaring above the lake, the sandy shore, and the road to town, Roserin worked her wings until the motion that moved her through the air became more natural. A mountain goat, scrabbling for food among the rocks, awoke a powerful hunger in her belly — as if she had not eaten in a hundred years. She resisted the urge to dive down and grab the beast, even though she could almost taste its blood and yearned to rip its flesh from its bones. She stayed her course, flying toward Farona as rapidly as she could move six wings.

Still, she could not fly swifter than the sun. With a raptor's vision, she could see the priests building a pyre of tinder-dry wood in the huge square in front of the massive stone temple. Roserin beat her wings faster. Two of the priests dragged Sethin — naked, his muscular arms bound to his sides, his ankles tied together — and laid him across the pyre. They had shaved off his beautiful hair and painted the sign of the phoenix in blood across his chest. Fear for his life and anger toward his abusers gave her strength to maintain a furious pace. Her cry pierced the silence that surrounded the village.

The priests, the cowls of their dark robes pulled down to hide their faces from the light, reacted by circling Sethin. They chanted and waved their torches about in an intricate pattern. Even from this distance, Roserin could see the panic on her son's face. The triangle under his right eye stood out dark against his pale skin. Roserin dove down, tucking in her massive wings to increase her speed. Priests threw back their cowls to stare at her, exposing their brown skin and coarse black hair. Several fled, the ceremonial words forgotten. A few flung themselves prostrate on the paving stones in front of their god incarnate.

Roserin circled Sethin who stared at her with incredulous blue eyes. The high priest, who wore a bronze medallion, mimicked a phoenix's keening and bowed to her. He shouted something she could not understand and two of those who still stood threw their torches on the pyre. Roserin hovered just above her son's bound body, her massive wingspan twice his height. Gripping one of Sethin's arms and one leg in her talons, Roserin lifted him from the flames. He coughed as the smoke from the burning pyre billowed up into his face. Several priests danced around the flames in a frenzy.

Circling above Farona, Roserin debated what to do next. She had brought the legend to life: a giant phoenix had stolen the offering from the sacrificial pyre. But Lukich's tale had ended there. Sethin trembled in her talons and she wished she had a voice with which to comfort him. She decided to take him to the Acasarn settlement on the other side of the mountain. She had heard that there only women served as priests and they never sacrificed human lives to honor their god, Rshbota. But would Acasarns treat fair-skinned folk as pariahs? And how would she return to her own form?

Roserin shuddered, remembering her body broken on the mountain slope and the pain she had known before waking as a phoenix. If she returned to her own form, would she still suffer those injuries, or would the magic that had transformed her also mend her broken bones? She had saved her son from the flames. But she still did not know how to remove the poison from the lake or take a woman's shape again.

The fear-surge that had given her the strength to carry Sethin away from the village ebbed before she reached the lake. When she passed near the summit of the mountain, weariness overwhelmed her. She decided to alight there and rest for a bit, perhaps comfort Sethin. She laid him down in front of the empty stone pedestal on the mountain's peak, tilted her head to examine his bindings, trying to determine how she could remove them without hurting him.

Sethin struggled to turn himself over so he faced her. "My god ... sage and sacred Tsorak ... thank you for saving me ..."

Roserin keened. Now her son believed the

Faronan's god had rescued him and she had no voice to explain his error.

Stone scraped against stone. Sethin rolled onto his back and turned his head toward the pedestal. A short, wizened man, hair the color of dirty snow hanging almost to his waist, stood in front of an opening in the massive stones. He held a small knife with a curved blade in his left hand. Roserin squawked a warning and craned her neck toward him, pressing her sharp beak against his arm. The man held out his hands, the knife resting across both palms. "This will cut the leather that binds your son, holy one." She lifted her beak from the man and watched him slice through the thongs that tied her son's arms and legs.

Sethin rubbed his wrists and flexed his fingers. "You call me Tsorak's son? Why? What's become of my mother?"

The old man nodded toward Roserin. "She stands before you."

Sethin stared at her, looked at the old man, and turned back to Roserin. She screeched, understanding, finally, the meaning of Lukich's words that she had recited when she prostrated herself on the altar. She hung her head, her beak resting on the feathers of her breast.

"Your mother promised the Tsorak anything it asked, and swore that if it saved your life, you would serve it." The old man laid his knife across Sethin's palms. "Tsorak requires that you take my place in the temple," he pointed to the opening in the pedestal, "and that your mother stand guard on the mountain."

The muscles in Sethin's face rippled and his lips pressed together in a thin line. He blinked and turned to the old man. "What? ... How? ... Why?"

The old man pointed to the empty pedestal. "No one alive transforms into the phoenix. When the Tsorak chooses another to stand guard, it releases the spirit of the last person who took its form. Only he who serves in the temple here survives to answer his successor's questions." A tear crept down the man's cheek and glistened from his unkempt beard. For the first time, Roserin noticed that a dark triangle marked the skin under his right eye. "My father climbed this mountain a hundred years ago, hoping to stop the priests from sacrificing me. I was but six at the time. His heart gave out after he pledged his service and as Tsorak he flew down to snatch me from the flames, as your mother did today."

"You've lived here alone since?"

The old man shook his head. "Because I was so young, the previous temple keeper stayed until he thought me old enough to understand my responsibilities. Until today, I've not exchanged a word with anyone since he left when I turned ten. The offerings from Faronans sustain us temple keepers and the curse of Tsorak keeps us alive until another releases us from its service."

"And my mother?" Tears coursed down Sethin's face.

"A snake tripped her and she broke her neck."

"The poison in the lake?" Sethin's voice sank to a whisper.

"Will probably disappear when the rains begin in a few weeks. My people call it the red tide. It rarely lasts more than a year or two."

Sethin sank to his knees on the stones. "What must I do?"

"Come, I will teach you." The old man turned and walked into the temple. Sethin stumbled to his feet and followed.

The sun was halfway between noon and sunset when they returned leading a bleating goat. With the old man's knife, Sethin slit the goat's throat and the two stepped back. Unable to resist the smell of blood, Roserin tore into the carcass with her beak, ripping away the flesh and tilting her head back to drop the meat down her gullet. When she had eaten all but the bones and the hide, Sethin reached out to stroke Roserin's bloody beak with his palm. "Thank you, Mother, for rescuing me. I'll never forget what you've sacrificed." He swallowed. "I promise to serve Tsorak, and you, as well as I can."

The hopeless look on Sethin's face, the grief in his voice, tore at Roserin's heart. Instead of saving his life, she had doomed him to immurement in Tsorak's temple, alone for a hundred years. She should have let him burn; at least then his torment would have only lasted a short while.

No! As long as he lives, he can hope.

The old man turned and walked the path that led down the mountain. Roserin watched him for a moment. She nuzzled the tip of her beak against her son's hand. Surely now that she had eaten, she had the strength to carry him away. She stretched her wings, but they weighed her down. She managed two beats, lifting herself only to the top of the pedestal. When her talons touched the flat rocks, they turned to stone. She struggled to free herself, but petrification crept up her legs and across her wings.

She prayed to the god of her childhood. "I beg you, Svinal, do not make my son suffer a hundred years. Send someone else to take his place before Sethin turns into a shriveled old man." But as her heart turned to stone, she realized that Svinal — only a myth in her memory — would not answer her prayer, just as Tsorak would not remove the poison from the lake.

The gods cared only for their own needs. The phoenix was just a stone statue on the top of a lonely mountain that every hundred years found a new guardian for its temple by taking the life of someone that guardian loved. Her final keen echoed across the valley.

P

Firestone

Jorane's survival depends on the Firestone, but will she reach it in time?

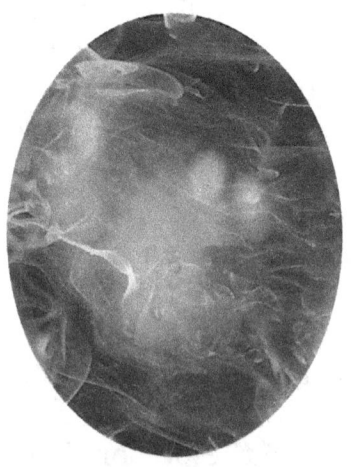

F.I. Goldhaber

Firestone

By F.I. Goldhaber

The steel bars, the stone floor, and the dank walls of the King's dungeon disappeared. Jorane projected herself back to the rocky precipice above Loncauver Bay, to the point on the bluff she had reached the day before. Waves crashed against the boulders below and she licked salt spray from her lips. Wrapping her arms around a protruding rock, she eased herself over the edge and searched with her toes to find purchase. She worked her way down the cliff side until she spotted the jewel — her mother's legacy — sparkling where the sunlight found it tucked deep in a crevice.

Metal clashed against metal as the door to her cell banged against the wall, the noise jerking her back once more to her cell in the King's dungeon. She wept, nausea washing over her, the disorientation caused by being wrenched back from the cliff exacerbating her grief over losing the opportunity to claim the gemstone. Today, for the first time since her mother's death, she had seen the Firestone. But only its touch would allow her to stay at Loncauver Bay. Until she reached the stone, any sound would yank her back to the dungeon's horrors.

The guard responsible for the clatter that forced her to lose her grip on the cliffs stooped under the low door, grabbed her thin arm, and dragged her out into the corridor. His fingers pressing into the flesh of her arm. Tears blurring her vision, Jorane stumbled behind him through a series of passageways. When he pulled her into the bright light of the courtyard, the touch of the sun burned her skin, and the pain caused her to faint. She woke to find herself face down against the cold slate floor, prone before the royal dais. Someone threw more water at her face, soaking her torn and filthy robes. She shivered.

"Wake up, Witch," a gruff voice shouted.

She wanted to ignore him, but a boot kicked into her ribs. Jorane pushed her bruised hands against the slate and lifted her head enough to glare at the guard who squatted over her, enjoying her torment.

"I believe she can answer your questions now, Majesty." The guard rose and stepped back.

Through dirty black hair spilling over her eyes, Jorane looked up at the two gilded thrones on the marble dais. His Royal Highness Lorrister, supreme ruler of Torrick and Vinser, reclined against the cushioned arm of the larger throne. He wore red velvet and satin raiments that did little to conceal a body hardened from years of wielding sword and battle axe. Thick red hair cushioned the jewel-encrusted gold crown that Lorrister had commissioned after he rode from his stronghold in the mountains of Slavold to invade Vinser ten years past.

To his left a kneeling female slave, naked but for a steel ring around her neck, balanced a platter of fruits on her head. Lorrister selected a large plum and stared at Jorane with pale blue eyes. He chewed slowly and Jorane's stomach growled.

"Where is it?" Lorrister's thick Slavoldian accent mimicked the eloquent and educated speech of the Vinser court.

"Where is what, Majesty?" Her voice quavered and she steadied herself, refusing to show weakness before the man who had conquered her homeland and enslaved her people.

Lorrister nodded at the guard who, gripped a handful of her hair, jerked her head back, and placed the flat of his sword against her throat.

"Do not play coy with me, Witch." Lorrister grabbed a handful of grapes and chewed through them. "The Firestone. Where is it?"

"Firestone? What is a Firestone, Majesty?"

Her scalp burned. Jorane used the pain to distance herself from the moment and to keep all thoughts of the gem's location from her mind where another witch might find it.

The guard tugged harder at her hair. She felt a small clump tear away, and the warm, sticky sensation of blood pooling on her scalp. The cold metal of the sword eased some of the pain from the burns on her skin.

"Majesty, you must have me confused with someone else. I'm no witch and I know nothing about a... stonefire."

The King spewed partially chewed grapes onto her upturned face, the seeds stinging her skin. A glob slid down her cheek and dripped from her chin onto her emaciated chest.

Lorrister's sister stepped out from the shadows behind his throne. Clouds of reddish blonde hair framed her narrow face. Blue eyes, set close together over a long, hooked nose, glared at Jorane. The rune for blood magic, carved from onyx, hung from a golden chain around Lorinona's neck. Thick red and black lines of forbidden sorcery ran through her aura.

"I have seen you leave your cell, Witch." Jorane felt the pull of the hypnotic spell Lorinona wove into her melodious voice.

Concentrating on her pain, Jorane emptied her mind of all thought. The witch might have seen Jorane disappear from her cell, but she could not have known to where she traveled.

"Don't play us for fools. If you tell us the

location of the Firestone, you'll die a quick and painless death. Otherwise, I promise we'll keep you alive to provide endless entertainment for His Majesty." She nodded at the King, then drifted to the second throne and seated herself.

"I almost hope she doesn't tell us," the King said. "Barratan claims to have some new tricks he wants to try out."

One side of Lorinona's mouth tilted upward and her eyes glistened. Jorane cringed, remembering legions of dead soldiers from both sides, resurrected by Lorinona's foul sorcery, attacking the Vinser and Torrick armies.

And Barratan had truly joined forces with a necromancer. Jorane winced. Until this moment, she had refused to believe her former teacher had betrayed the witches' league, even though others said he was the one who had murdered her mother. Has Barratan told the King who I am? Or does he fear revealing his own past? She thought about invoking the spell that would stop her heart, but she had gotten so close to the stone this last projection.

Languishing in her cell for weeks until the King returned from her homeland, Torrick, she had only managed to escape for an hour or so each day to follow the trail her mother had left for her. Now, she needed but a few moments alone to climb down that last bit and reach the stone that would allow her to fight the tyrant. Without it, Jorane could not hope to invoke magic strong enough to harm Lorrister as long as his sister's power protected him.

Surely, they could not subject her to anything worse than she had already endured. Swallowing, she said: "Then, you get your wish, Majesty, for I know nothing about any stone-fire."

The King waved at the guard, who dragged Jorane across the room by her remaining hair. Her feet scrabbled trying to find purchase on the polished slate and take some of the stress off her bleeding scalp. Stopping where manacles dangled at the ends of chains through a metal ring in the ceiling, the guard forced her wrists into the shackles. The chains tightened as a second guard turned the wheel affixed to the stone wall, tightening the chain until Jorane's feet cleared the floor by several inches. She swayed back and forth, her full weight pulling at her shoulders and wrists. The first guard locked another set of manacles on her ankles and secured the chain through a matching ring on the floor. She closed her eyes, tears seeping out, caused as much by the despair in her heart as the pain in her body.

The illusion of smoke and fire erupted in front of her. When the cloud vanished, Barratan appeared, his gold-embroidered scarlet robes billowing around him. A gold circlet held the blood magic rune, carved from obsidian, on his forehead. Jorane stared into the cold grey eyes in which she had once sought comfort and understanding. Then his white hair, long beard, and lined face had represented the epitome of kindness and knowledge.

He waved his hand in front of her chest. Pain started in her toes, traveled up her legs, and enveloped her body. The coarse fabric of her tattered clothing burst into flames and Jorane screamed in agony. She tried to turn the magic away, but Barratan had too much power. Desperate to end the pain, Jorane finally gave up all hope and spoke the spell that should have stopped her heart. But, the magic did not answer her call. The pain continued to burn away her skin, incinerate her flesh, and scorch her very bones. She recognized the touch of Barratan's magic preventing her from fainting, keeping her alive. She longed for the Firestone, but refused to call its location to her mind.

The pain stopped as quickly as it had begun. Jorane looked down, expecting to see charred skin and instead found her gaunt body still covered by ragged robes. She hung limply in her restraints.

Lorinona stood next to Barratan, chuckling. Jorane reached for her magic, but encountered only a black wall. She would never touch her legacy and avenge her mother's death. She could not stop her heart or even invoke a simple spell to ease some of the pain. Jorane sobbed.

The two sorcerers laughed at her tears. "We've only just started, foolish girl." Stepping close, Barratan whispered in her ear. "You will regret your refusal to join me."

She shook her head. Barratan's betrayal destroyed her mother, Jilissi, and everything the witches' league had accomplished in a hundred years. Her one-time teacher had tried to convince Jilissi that Lorrister represented the future. Barratan claimed uniting the kingdoms would bring more prosperity than the witches ever could. Jilissi had sacrificed her life to keep the King from acquiring the Firestone. Jorane, the last of Jilissi's daughters, had promised her mother's ghost she would retrieve the Firestone and use it to avenge Jilissi's death.

Barratan swept his arms in a circle. Lorinona just stared at Jorane. Both sorcerers sent pain searing through her limbs.

"Ingenious application of body and mind magic, my dear." He spoke to Lorinona, but Jorane guessed he intended his words for her ears. "True torture leaves such grievous wounds and forces one to wait for the subject to recover between questionings."

Jorane opened her mouth to scream, but nothing emerged and her throat closed.

"Directly stimulating the nerves produces the same sensations, without marking the body or damaging the heart and lungs."

The pain eased and Jorane fell limp in her bonds.

Lorinona's fingers stroked the skin of Jorane's back and blades plunged into her, cutting through her flesh. The sorceress turned her hand and the blades' dull edges severed the muscles of Jorane's back. Wet warmth spilled down across her ass. A tormented howl, more animal than human, tore from her throat.

Lorinona stepped back and the wounds vanished. Jorane swayed, her body drenched only in sweat.

Barratan snickered, gripping her head. Iron bands encircled her brow and descended over her eyes. With a rusty creak of a crank, the bands constricted until she felt the crack of bone. Blood filled her eye sockets, falling down her face like tears. Her eyes. They had blinded her.

Barratan released her. She blinked. She could see.

The iron scent of blood enveloped her from behind and her former teacher whispered in her ear. "I have as many torments for you as I have imagination and you will remember each and ever one in vivid detail for what remains of your life. We will continue torturing you," his voice rose to fill the throne room and echo off the walls, "until you tell me where the stone is, traitorous daughter of a whore!" He lowered his voice to a whisper again. "Spare yourself the agony. Allow yourself to die with as much dignity remains to you, while you still have your mind. If you don't tell me where to find the stone, I will render you into a madwoman for the King to keep chained to his throne gibbering and howling, so all who might disobey him will know the price of resistance."

Tears streamed down her face, but she shook her head.

"So be it." He gripped the sides of her neck. "And again."

Lorinona drew her fingers in front of Jorane's eyes and she screamed.

The two of them flayed every inch of her body, broke her bones, and crushed her joints. They tore her limbs from their sockets. She drowned. She burned. She hung from the neck.

Hours passed. Days? At some point she noticed the King's throne empty, but she couldn't say when. She lost track of time, her tongue swollen with thirst, her mouth parched, her lips cracked.

Lorinona yawned and Barratan sighed. "As pleasant and memorable as this day has been my dear student, we require rest. Do not despair, though. We will return in the morning." He gestured toward the guards. "Keep watch." Barratan vanished into billows of smoke. Lorinona simply disappeared.

Jorane's chin rested on her chest. Her body swayed in the shackles, her fingers numb, her shoulders aching, her wrists and ankles raw from the manacles' chafing, and her spirit bleeding. How long? How long could she hold out before she revealed the Firestone's location just to make the pain stop?

A vision of Lorrister, wearing the gem on a

platinum chain around his neck, twisted her empty gut and brought bile to her throat. She tried to remember when they had last given her food or water. Mayhap she could die of thirst or starvation before she told them where to find the Firestone. But that hope faded with the knowledge that Barratan and Lorinona could use magic to keep her alive, even without feeding her, until they got what the King wanted.

One by one, the guards, knowing her body too frail to escape her restraints, deserted the throne room to seek sustenance and sleep.

The Firestone would give Lorrister the power to enslave every witch in the world. No one would have magic enough to defy him. He would add Ritnorak in the south and Shiloston in the east to his conquests. Thousands would die, and his armies would enslave thousands more. Agonized voices from the future ripped Jorane's heart apart.

If only...

But she was just one of a few dozen witches left in the league. Hundreds had died in futile efforts to defend Vinser and Torrick from Lorrister's soldiers and Lorinona's magic. Many of those who survived had abandoned the league and followed Barratan when he joined the King. Barratan convinced many witches they could accomplish more working with Lorrister than fighting against him. But they had not seen the haunted eyes of women raped by Lorrister's soldiers, the bodies of children his soldiers had sliced open. The witches who followed Barratan had not known the despair of slavery, the anguish of watching their sons molded into soldiers for Lorrister's army. Jorane shut out the pain. Those women, those men, those parents had pleaded with her mother and the witches' league for aid. They had no one else to stand between them and Lorrister's plan to unify the world under his banner.

Jorane gritted her teeth. No one else could retrieve the stone and stand up to Lorrister. She had to try. In her mind's eye, she focused on the gem where it nestled in the rock opening on the side of the cliff, visible only to the moon at night and to the shore birds that swooped in the air during the day. She concentrated on the gem: she could see the fire within the clear, green stone the size of her eye and its polished surface shimmered in the moonlight. If it rested in the middle of her palm, its heat would penetrate her skin, the smooth surface would tingle against her fingertips. The stone would give her the power to do more than seek vengeance. With it, she could unite the remaining witches, lure back enough to start a rebellion in Torrick, and help defend Ritnorak. She could win not only her freedom, but that of thousands who now had no hope.

The wind tugged at her rags and chilled Jorane's skin. Salt spray coated her legs. Her fingers and toes clung to the rocks. Barratan and Lorinona had not severed her connection to the

Firestone after all. Jorane suppressed her joy and relief, for she still needed to touch the stone before anyone returned to the throne room. Her position allowed her to look into the crevice, although she must move along the cliff face before she could reach inside it. Jorane's heart skipped a beat. She could not see the stone. The full moon lit the wave peaks below with an eerie glow and the stone should reflect the light as it had in her vision. Jorane found purchase, moved closer to the crevice, and stuck her arm inside. Although she ran her hand across every rocky surface, cutting her fingers on sharp edges, she could not touch the stone. Her breath caught in her throat. Had someone else retrieved it, someone who would take it to Lorrister?

But, she could still sense its power. It must be near. Her wrists no longer bled or even ached from the chafing caused by the hours she had spent hanging in shackles. Her shoulders no longer throbbed and she could move her fingers again. Her scalp felt whole and all of her hair whipped about in the wind. The pain that had permeated her body had vanished, taking with it some of her despair.

Dawn tinged the edge of the sky, and in her mind's eye Jorane could see the guards returning to the throne room. She should just let go, fall to her death and prevent the sorcerers from torturing her further. If someone had taken the Firestone, she had nothing to live for, no hope of defeating Lorrister. Lorinona and Barratan would continue tormenting her until she lost her mind.

The guards shouted and more soldiers trooped into the throne room. Jorane almost opened her fingers — almost let herself fall to her death — when the realization that she still clung to the cliff face penetrated her panic. Without the Firestone's touch, the noise of the first guard's arrival should have dragged her back to her restraints. She allowed herself to hope.

Jorane pulled herself up to the plateau, taken aback by the strength in her arms. Standing on the rocky expanse inhabited only by shorebirds, she watched the sun rise. She stayed near the cliff edge, ready to jump before anything could pull her back to Lorrister's palace a thousand leagues away. The power of the Firestone still seemed close enough to touch, but she could not see it anywhere on the plateau. And, who would climb down the cliff, retrieve the stone, and then leave it lying about?

Barratan stormed into the throne room and screamed at the guards, his face red, his spittle spraying those nearest him. He stood in front of the chains that should have held Jorane's tortured body. Eyes blazing, he cast spells of capture, retrieval, and possession making grand gestures and shouting the words that most witches whispered. Lorinona joined him and Jorane's vision showed their magic weaving together in tendrils of black and red. She countered each spell with power drawn from the Firestone and reveled in the warmth of the sun on her skin.

She smiled. For the first time in her life, the sun's touch did not burn. Jorane put her hand on her forehead to caress the Firestone's smooth face. She rejoiced at the tingling of magic that permeated her fingers and laughed and laughed.

The stone she had chased since her mother's death, that had eluded her efforts for nearly a year, had come to her when she accepted the responsibility that it brought with it. Joy flooded through her, chasing away even the memory of the pain inflicted by the two left behind to face the King's wrath.

Whole at last, she reached out with the magic of her mother and her mother's mother and caused a monstrous ball of fire to blaze through Lorrister's throne room. Guards doused it with water, to no avail, then fled for their lives, their clothing igniting as they ran. The flames destroyed the thrones and scorched the dais. Even if the King built new ones, the ashes would leave an indelible black mark to remind Lorrister, Lorinona, and Barratan of her power.

She pushed the vision from her mind. Jorane did not need to witness Barratan's rage, Lorinona's fury, or Lorrister's terror to know they understood her meaning. The Firestone had accepted her promise to help the people of

Vinser and Torrick, of Ritnorak and Shiloston. It had affixed itself to the forehead of its chosen witch and would stay there as long as she lived.

With a word, Jorane replaced the rags she wore with long flowing robes of midnight black silk. She longed for a bath in hot water, a meal of meat without maggots, bread without mold, and a bottle of good Torrick wine. But first she must rekindle the battle that had taken her mother's life. The witches had scattered at Jilissi's death, those who did not follow Barratan into the King's service fleeing to hide to the shelter of obscurity. Jorane must convince them to rally to the Firestone's choice and bring them back into the league. Only together would they have enough power to defeat Lorrister and free Torrick and Vinser.

Jorane stood tall in the morning light and promised the warm sun that the King would rue the day he directed Barratan to kill Jilissi so he could steal the Firestone. But, she assured the gem, when the witches agreed to follow her, she would no longer make avenging her mother's death her primary purpose. With a calm surety that reminded her of her mother's serene approach to life, Jorane accepted her responsibility to lead the witches in revolt against Lorrister and save people from his tyranny. Eventually, vengeance would just add sweetness to her efforts.

𝔍

Also by F.I. Goldhaber:

Fiction:

Ticket to Faerie

Stranger Than Fiction

Rebellion

Evolution

Chasing Time

Destiny

Dragon Treasure

Finding Magic

Poetry:

Subversive Verse

Pairs of Poems